nickelodeon

Sunny Day

⋆˙⋆ Pop Star Makeover! ⋆˙⋆

Adapted by **Mickey Matheis**

Illustrated by **Miranda Yeo**

A Random House PICTUREBACK® Book

Random House 🏠 New York

© 2018 Viacom International Inc. All rights reserved. Published in the United States by Random House Children's Books, a division of Penguin Random House LLC, 1745 Broadway, New York, NY 10019, and in Canada by Penguin Random House Canada Limited, Toronto. Pictureback, Random House, and the Random House colophon are registered trademarks of Penguin Random House LLC. Nickelodeon, Nick Jr., Sunny Day, and all related titles, logos, and characters are trademarks of Viacom International Inc.
rhcbooks.com
ISBN 978-0-525-57771-3
Printed in the United States of America
10 9 8 7 6 5 4 3 2 1

Sunny and her friends Rox and Blair were excited. Their favorite pop star was on her way to Sunny's Salon!

"I can't believe Mandy is coming *here* to get her hair done for her new music video!" exclaimed Blair.

Sunny's dog, Doodle, couldn't wait. He was a superfan!

"I love Mandy's new song, 'Rainbow Kind of Day,'" Doodle said as he danced, singing the catchy tune.

"Did you order that special Pop Star Purple hair chalk?" Sunny asked Rox. "We'll need them to give Mandy her makeover."

"Yep!" Rox replied. "Should be here any minute now!"

"The mail was supposed to arrive thirty minutes ago," said Blair.

Sunny and Doodle went to find the mail carrier.
When they stepped outside, they nearly ran into their
friend Timmy, who was helping deliver the mail.
   "Watch out!" he yelled.
   CRASH! Packages went flying everywhere!

Sunny made sure Timmy was okay. Then she asked if he had a package for her.

"Yes," said Timmy. He searched the pile of boxes—but all the labels had fallen off! He had deliveries for Sunny, Lacey, Cindy, and Peter, but he didn't know which was which.

"I've got this," Doodle announced. "I'm an excellent sniffer dog." He sniffed all the packages and chose one. "This is definitely hair chalk."

But when Sunny opened the box back at her salon, she found green foam bricks.

"It looks like we got the wrong package!" she said.

Sunny thought maybe the person who'd ordered the bricks got her package instead.

"You know," she said, "I think I've seen these green bricks before. I know who they belong to!"

Sunny led her friends to the Glam Van. They all jumped in.

The friends zoomed over to Peter's Flower Shop.
His usually tidy shop was very messy—and he was
twisted up in a huge vine!
"A little help?" he asked.

"Good thing I always have my detangling comb with me," Sunny said, freeing Peter in no time. Then she handed him the green bricks.

Peter was thrilled! He had ordered the bricks to help him arrange flowers. He could finally finish the bouquets he'd been making for Princesses Annabella and Dominica—and then organize his shop!

"Any chance you got our package?" Sunny asked hopefully. Peter handed her a box containing different-sized cups. "I'm afraid not," he said, "but I did get these funny-shaped cups."

"Maybe whoever ordered these cups has our chalk," said Sunny.

Back in the Glam Van, Sunny noticed lines
and numbers on the cups. "These are measuring
cups—like a baker would use," she said.
"Cindy's a baker!" Blair pointed out.
The group headed to the bakery.

The friends arrived at the bakery—where a big mixer was splattering batter all over the shop!

Sunny pulled a large hair cape from her apron. She opened it to catch the flying batter. Rox dove toward the out-of-control mixer and turned it off.

"Thanks!" Cindy said. "It's been one cupcake catastrophe after another today."

"I can't seem to get the amount of ingredients right," Cindy explained. "If only I had those measuring cups I ordered!"

When Sunny handed Cindy the box with the cups, her face lit up. Now she could finish her big cupcake order!

Cindy gave Sunny the dog collar she'd received by mistake. It said "KC" on it. Sunny and her friends knew who it belonged to! They sped over to Lacey's house.

Sunny gasped when Lacey opened her front door. She had bright purple hair, and the chalk box was on a table behind her!

"That purple hair chalk was meant for the salon!" Sunny told her. "You can't just take other people's belongings."

"Well, you've got KC's collar!" Lacey replied, grabbing it and slamming the door.

Sunny knew how she could get her hair chalk.

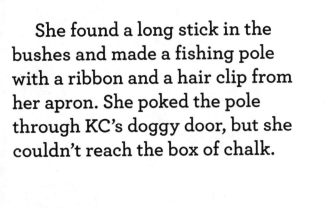

She found a long stick in the bushes and made a fishing pole with a ribbon and a hair clip from her apron. She poked the pole through KC's doggy door, but she couldn't reach the box of chalk.

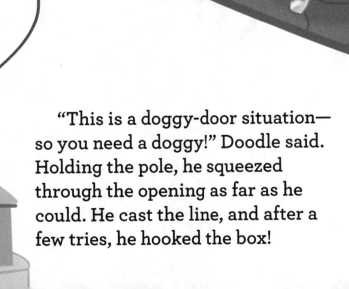

"This is a doggy-door situation—so you need a doggy!" Doodle said. Holding the pole, he squeezed through the opening as far as he could. He cast the line, and after a few tries, he hooked the box!

Once again, the girls and Doodle piled into the Glam Van.

"Finally! Our Pop Star Purple hair chalk!" Rox said, opening the box.

They couldn't believe their eyes.

The box was empty!

They looked out the van window and saw Lacey leaving her house with KC. The dog's fur was totally purple! Sunny knew at once that Lacey and KC has used up all their chalk.

"That's it," Blair said sadly. "We'll just have to tell Mandy that we won't be able to give her Pop Star Purple hair after all. . . ."

The friends returned to the salon.

Sunny refused to give up. She asked Rox and Blair to help her search for any extra bits of chalk they could find. Just then, Peter arrived with flowers. Cindy soon followed with cupcakes. They wanted to thank Sunny for her help.

As Sunny listened to her friends sing "Rainbow Kind of Day," she looked at the assorted hair chalks, flowers, and festive cupcakes.

She had an amazing idea. And it was just in time. . . .

"Hello?" a friendly voice called from the
front door of the salon. Mandy!

"We've had a little trouble today," Sunny said.
She admitted that they didn't have the Pop Star
Purple hair chalk. "But we've got something
even better for you, with *all* the colors!"

"All the colors?" Mandy said. "Like a rainbow?"

"Just like your song!" Sunny said, and she pointed at the different pieces of chalk.

"I love it!" Mandy exclaimed. "This is way better than just Pop Star Purple!"

Sunny showed Mandy several hairstyles on her tablet. The singer wanted to try the Pop Star Pinwheels look.

"Great choice!" Sunny said approvingly.

"And I'll give you a rainbow-colored manicure to match," Blair added.

Mandy loved her makeover! "Nothing says 'Rainbow Kind of Day' like my hair!"

In fact, Mandy was so happy that she decided to shoot her music video right there in Sunny's Salon. And she invited Sunny and her friends to be in it!

Just then, Timmy, who had volunteered to film the video, arrived with his camera.

"And . . . action!" Timmy said.

Sunny and her friends danced and sang along with Mandy. They couldn't believe they were actually in her video!

This was definitely a day for the Style Files!